Tall Tales

E.R.Reilly

Illustrated by
Janet Bates

PUBLISHED IN GREAT BRITAIN BY
SANTIAGO PRESS
PO BOX 8808
BIRMINGHAM
B30 2LR
E-mail for orders and enquiries: santiago@reilly19.freeserve.co.uk

Reprinted 2010, 2011

ISBN 0-9539229-4-4

Printed and bound in India by
OM Authentic Media, P.O. Box 2190, Secunderabad 500 003
E-mail: printing@ombooks.org

This book is based upon a short
story that my mum wrote.
I dedicate it to her memory.

Eámonn

To Dad - Forever in my heart.
Janet

Tall Tales

We sit on a carpet during literacy hour in our class. On a Monday morning we sit there for Show-and-Tell as well. Our teacher asked us if we wanted to tell about our holidays. My hand was the first one to shoot up in the air because I love to tell stories. Telling stories is my favourite thing to do in the whole world. Miss didn't ask me to tell straight away. I know why she doesn't like to choose me. You see, I have a habit of telling tall tales. I know that it's a wrong thing to do, but I just can't stop myself. Don't get me wrong; I don't tell tall tales all of the time.

It's just that, from time to time, a tall tale just comes out of my mouth without me even thinking about it.

I waved my hand about as though my life depended on it and shouted, "Miss! Miss!"

In the end, she asked me to tell my story.

My dad took me and my little brother, Josh, to Europe for our summer holiday. My name is Tanya, by the way. Because of my little habit of telling tall tales, people sometimes call me Tanya Tall Tales. I don't mind it when they call me that. It's my own fault really. I wish people didn't think that I tell tall tales all the time, because I don't. Not all the time.

Europe was great. We went potholing. I wasn't very keen at first. To be honest, I get a bit frightened in the dark. It wasn't that dark to begin with. You don't have to do much climbing down for the first half an hour or so. You have a helmet on that has a torch on it, so that stops you from feeling that you are completely in the dark. Josh is quite small, so Dad kept a close eye on him all of the time. There were about twenty of us altogether. I was one of the last. There was nothing too difficult; to begin with we gradually climbed deeper and deeper down into the cave. You could tell that you were getting deeper underground because the passageways got tighter and more difficult to get through and it got a lot colder.

I was lagging behind a bit because I had my headphones on. I wasn't taking as much notice as I should have been and I ended up going down the wrong passageway. By the time that I realised that that I had got split up from the others, I was completely on my own. I had lost track of how long I had been on my own. I took my headphones off and shouted for help, but there was no response. It was very dark and there was a lot of water on

the ground. There were some stalactites hanging from the top of the rocks as well. It was extremely cold and more than a bit frightening, I can tell you. I couldn't tell which passageways I had taken to get where I was, and so I had no way of knowing if I was going in the right direction to get back to the others, or if I was going further away from them. I just kept on the way that I was going and hoped that I would see or hear them before too long.

The passageway in front of me got very tight. The rocks were sticking out in an awkward way and I could see that I would have some difficulty crawling past them, but I could see that there was a much bigger passageway just around the corner. So I pressed on and forced my way through. The only problem was that the new passageway was a dead end. I was in a tricky position because I had nowhere to go forward. I had to go backwards. There was no choice in that. The only choice I had was whether I should try and turn round in the small space I was in or crawl backwards through the gap that I had first squeezed through. The only problem with going backwards was that I would have to stay going backwards for about twenty metres. I decided that I would do my best to turn round.

I pulled on the rock in front of me to try and drag myself up. To my absolute amazement, the rock creaked backwards and a huge great opening became visible in front of me. There before me was the brightest and biggest room that I had ever seen. I couldn't believe my eyes. There were hundreds of small men in smart, brightly coloured suits. All of them were busy working, but, when the rock opened up, they all stopped to look at me. I just stood and stared at them and they just stood and stared back. I rubbed my eyes and looked again. It was amazing. It was astonishing. I had never dreamt that anything like this ever existed.

One of the small people came running up to me. He wasn't a child. He was an adult but he was just smaller than adults usually are. As he got closer to me, his eyes lit up and he threw his arms into the air. He shouted to all of his friends to tell them that I was human. Then he came closer and shouted that I was a human child. When he told them that I was a human girl, they all cheered. He said that they hadn't seen a human girl in over a thousand years. It was a fantastic sight. All of the small people were jumping up and down and hugging each other and dancing.

I told them that I got split up from my dad and my little brother, Josh, and lots of other people. I told them that I needed to get back to them or they would be worried. The small people laughed and told me not to worry. They said that it didn't matter how long I spent with them. When they returned me back to Dad and the others it would only seem as though I had been missing for a few seconds. They were all so very friendly; I just knew that they must have been telling the truth. I seemed to relax straight away. I don't know why but I knew I was in a safe place and that I was among new friends.

The first of the small people to come and greet me was called BB. He showed me all around and told me about his world. I introduced myself to him and we shook hands. BB was brilliant. He was a checker. His people were called Alphas. They lived underground in the caves. They never ventured out of their land except for the rarest of emergencies. BB didn't think that any Alpha had left their world for well over five hundred years. He turned to the other Alphas nearby and asked them if they could think of an Alpha having to go up to Earth recently. A group of about ten to fifteen little

Alphas formed themselves into a little huddle and they all talked away at the same time for a while until suddenly they all stopped and stood up and turned back to face us. An Alpha called QB spoke up.

He said, "No, no, none of us can think of an Alpha leaving Alphaworld for over a thousand years."

All of the Alphas began talking at once again and they said things like, "Yes, yes. He's quite right. Quite right. Not for over a thousand years."

They all stopped again and looked at me. I didn't know what to do so I just smiled at them all.

"Oh, isn't she lovely!" QB said, and all of the others agreed. "Yes, yes. Quite lovely. Oh, yes. She has the sweetest smile that you could possibly wish for."

BB walked me down the steps to get closer to all of the other Alphas. He held onto my hand and hugged my arm.

"This is Tanya," he told them.

They all came forward to meet me. One by one they shook my hand and hugged my arm, or they held my hand up to their face. Some of them wanted to snuggle up for a bit too long, so BB hurried them along.

"Honestly," he said. "Anybody would think that you've never seen a little girl before."

"But we haven't," they told him.

"Oh, dear me, yes. Oh, yes. Quite right. Yes, yes, quite right," BB said.

He told me that he had forgotten how young some of the youngsters were. He said some of them were only a few hundred years old, so we should make allowances for them. BB realised that all of this was as big a shock for me as it was for all of the Alphas. He asked me to come over and sit down. He led me to a little wooden chair and I sat down. I felt very scruffy compared to all of the Alphas. I sat there with my boots and jeans and my orange jacket and my helmet. I took my helmet off and put it on my lap.

BB lifted up the tails of his bright yellow jacket and he sat down beside me. He put one leg across the other and sat back in his chair. His boots were made of bright patent leather and they had buckles that shone with bright diamonds. He stroked his long white beard and flicked his long white hair over his shoulders. He told me that he would show me around Alphaworld and tell me all about it, presently. He told me that I should rest first and that I should ask him questions, if I had any.

As you can imagine, I had about a hundred million questions to ask. My problem was thinking about where to start. I began by asking about my dad and my little brother, Josh. BB told me not to worry. In Alphaworld, time has little meaning. It certainly doesn't mean anything like it does up on the Earth. BB assured me that when they put me back into the cave, my dad and my brother would think that I had only been missing for a few seconds. Somehow I just knew that I could trust him and so I relaxed again. He wouldn't need to explain it to me anymore. I knew that Dad and Josh wouldn't be worrying about me. I asked BB where they all got their beautiful clothes from. Do you know, they made them all themselves?

Some of the Alphas were tailors. They designed and made all of the Alphas' beautiful clothes. They all wore brightly coloured suits stitched with pure gold thread, and their shirts were made with ruffles and bows. All Alphas have beautiful long hair and tie it up with ribbons that match their suits.

A very energetic young Alpha stepped forward and did a little dance. He did a little tap dance and then he jumped in the air and clicked his heels together. He gave me a big bow and then he stood up straight and held onto the lapels of his jacket. BB introduced him to me. He was called DB and he was the best shoemaker in all of

Alphaworld. DB's face beamed with the biggest smile that you have ever seen in your life. The group of Alphas in front of me all moved out of the way to allow some new Alphas to walk in. They were the Alpha chefs.

One of them called out to BB and said, "We thought that Miss Tanya would like something to eat and drink."

Another chef joined in with him. "Yes, yes, something to eat and drink. We thought that Miss Tanya might like some food."

BB jumped up from his chair. "Jolly good thinking," he said. "Yes, yes, jolly good thinking. Well done. Yes, very well done indeed."

Twenty Alpha chefs lined up to offer me food that was fit for a queen. They each carried silver trays that were heaped high with all of the most fabulous food that you could ever dream of. I could tell that each of the Alpha chefs was hoping that I would choose their tray to eat from. I decided to eat a little from every tray to try and keep them all happy. I'm a vegetarian and I was in luck because all Alpha food was vegetarian. I was given a silver spoon to eat with and I walked about the Alpha chefs taking a spoonful of food from each of their trays. I ate mashed potato with beans and tomato sauce. I ate veggie sausages with a barbeque sauce. I ate spicy nuggets and veggie burger and chips and then I moved onto puddings and I took a huge spoonful of wobbly blancmange and a slice of fruit cake with icing on and then I finished by eating a great big spoonful of trifle with cream. The Alpha who was holding the trifle tray looked especially pleased that I particularly liked his food. I took another spoonful and the Alpha who held the tray was so pleased he did a little jig.

BB handed me a beautiful golden goblet and I took a long drink of the most delicious fruit juice that I had tasted in my life. All of the Alphas

smiled when they saw how much I liked it. They all started talking at once.

"Oh, yes, yes, Miss Tanya. We thought that you would like it. Yes, yes, it's our own recipe you know. Yes, yes, it's quite delicious, isn't it? You wouldn't find anything nearly as nice up on the Earth you know! No, no, no, you can only get this in Alphaworld."

I told them that it was the most beautiful drink that I had ever tasted in my life. All of the Alpha chefs hugged each other and the other Alphas gave them a big clap. I hadn't told a tall tale though. It *was* the most beautiful drink that I had ever drunk in my entire life.

BB took my hand. He said. "Yes, yes. That's very good indeed. Very good, but now you must see what Alphaworld is really all about."

All of the Alphas smiled and clapped as BB led me towards the huge workshop that was Alphaworld. As far as I could see, there were long rows of little Alphas working at benches. They were busy making toys. There were large toys and small toys and some in between. There were toys for the twenty-first century and there were old-fashioned little toys made from wood. The Alphas sang songs and whistled tunes as they worked. BB was a checker. That means that he checked toys to make sure that they were all of the very highest quality. Although he was supposed to be showing me around rather than working, he couldn't stop himself from picking up toys from time to time and inspecting them. When he picked up a small china vase to go in a toy home it was a bit small for him to check. BB took a miniature magnifying glass from his top pocket and looked at the vase closely. The Alphas who were working on the toy house section stopped and stared at BB. They looked a bit worried, to be honest. Then BB nodded his head.

"Yes, yes, very good," they said to each other.

"Yes, yes. Very good indeed," they said again, and they tittered and laughed.

We carried on walking around Alphaworld. I was astonished to see so many Alphas making so many toys.

I asked BB who all of the toys were for and he said, "Yes, yes, I rather thought you might ask that. Yes, yes, well, you are one of the first ever children to stumble into Alphaworld. Yes, yes, I rather thought you would ask that. Yes, yes, well, these toys are for you. Well, that is to say, no, no, they're not for you. They're for children. Human children, just like you. They are for all children everywhere. They are for all the children of the Earth from every century. Yes, yes, all children."

I couldn't quite understand what was happening. All of the Alphas turned together and waved and shouted, "Hello! Hello!" A big part of the wall opened up and Alphas started passing toys of all description through to an old man dressed in red who had a long white beard.

I said, "Is that ...?"

BB said, "Um, yes, yes, quite. Umm, yes, yes."

I asked if I could go and see him, but BB said it was out of the question because he was too busy.

"No, no, no," he said. "That's quite out of the question. He's far busier than any Alpha. He lives in Alpha years, but he works in Earth years. Yes, yes, human Earth children only get to know that he has visited them on Christmas Eve, but it takes him all year to visit every single child on Earth. The only day that he gets off is Christmas Day. Yes, yes. He comes down to Alphaworld and we have a big comfy chair for him and we pull his boots off. Yes, yes, pull his boots off. Yes. Ha! Ha! Yes, yes, we pull his boots off and then he likes to soak his feet in a big bowl of soapy water and then the Alpha chefs prepare him a super feast. Yes, yes, super, yes, a super feast. Ha! Ha!"

I couldn't wait to get back to Josh to tell him about my adventure. BB understood and brought me to a new hole in the wall.

"Yes, yes, we quite understand, Tanya. Yes, yes, we quite understand. We knew that you would want to get back. We quite understand, yes, quite, quite."

I turned round to take one last look at Alphaworld and every single Alpha had stopped work to look at me. I waved goodbye and I could see all of the Alphas were sad. Some even took handkerchiefs out of their pockets or from up their sleeves and gave their eyes a wipe.

"Goodbye, Alphas." I said.

They all said goodbye with very sad and soft voices. Then I turned to BB and said a special goodbye to him. I bent down and gave him a big hug. BB stroked his beard and looked rather coy. He turned round to look at the other Alphas and they all smiled at each other.

I walked through the hole in the wall and made my way round the corner. There in front of me were Dad and Josh.

"Come on," Dad said. "Make sure you keep up."

I turned round to look back at the Alphas, but their whole world had become blocked up again. All that was there was a normal cave wall. I stepped back to push it open to say one last goodbye, but the rock wouldn't budge. It was just a normal rock.

My teacher clapped her hands and all the children joined in. She said that I told a very interesting tale as usual but she said that she wanted to know what really happened on our holidays. That's something that I have to put up with. Because I do occasionally tell tall tales, people think that I'm telling tall tales all of the time. Mind you, Josh didn't help. He told his teacher that we went on holiday in a caravan to Skegness. They all believed him. Everybody believes Josh. But, you see, Josh doesn't tell tall tales so that's why people believe him all the time. Anyway, Josh and I are lucky because we have two holidays. Our parents live apart now.

We still live in our old house with our mum, but we live with our dad in his flat as well. Dad lives in a flat in another part of the city. It takes just over half an hour to get there. We go to school on a Wednesday morning from our mum's house and when we leave school on a Wednesday, we go to Dad's flat. We stay at our dad's house until Saturday lunch time and then go to Mum's house. This means that we spend half of the week with Mum and half of the week with Dad. I know a lot of kids spend one week with one parent and the next week with the other, but this really suits us.

Mum's house is good. It's where we have always been. Mum has got a new partner now. His name is Jimmy. We like him, but he's not perfect. He can be nice some of the time. There are times when he wants to start playing games and then he just stops. You can be right in the middle of a game and then he just decides that he wants to stop and doesn't matter what me and Josh want. We have to stop there and then. When we are on holiday, we have to do whatever he wants. Last year, we went to Burnham-on-Sea. There was a big leisure park there with hundreds of caravans and tents. There were two big swimming pools with five big slides and there was a fairground there. In the evenings, there was entertainment in the lounge. Josh and I really liked that. You get to do lots of dancing and shouting out and you get to enter competitions and they have magic acts on and there are Slush Puppies. It's really good. We had been there for about three nights and then Jimmy said that we had to go for a walk instead. Me and Josh told Mum that we wanted to go to the club but she said that we had to go for a walk. She would never have made us do that if Jimmy wasn't there, and Dad would never have made us go for a walk if we had told him that we wanted to go to the club. I'm not trying to say that he's really bad because he's not. We really do like him most of the time. Mum

40

likes him, and Josh and I want her to be happy. It's just that he's the kind of person that has to get his own way all of the time. I suppose I'm a bit like that as well, to be honest.

Actually, it was really funny when we went on holiday, because we went horse riding. Mum's horse, my horse and Josh's horse would all do what we wanted them to do, but Jimmy couldn't make his horse do anything at all. There was a woman who was walking with us and Jimmy's horse did whatever she told her to.

So everybody could make the horses do whatever they wanted them to, except Jimmy. It was driving him

mad. He kept telling his horse to walk on but she just stood still. We took no notice at first, but the more he tried to get his horse to do things, the more she ignored him. He sat there saying "walk on" or "giddy up" and she just stood there, eating a hedge. Josh and I were looking at each other and smiling. Then Mum saw us and she couldn't stop herself smiling and, in the end, we all burst out laughing and that made Jimmy really mad. So he started being really firm with his horse and started pulling her away from the hedge really quite roughly. But the horse just stood there ignoring him. Then he shouted at her to walk away at once but the horse just stood there and did a wee. This made us laugh even more. Josh was rocking backwards and forwards so much on his saddle that I

thought he was going to fall off. Then Jimmy told the horse to move on at once. He told the horse that her behaviour was intolerable, but the horse just stood there eating and refused to move. We were all laughing so much our stomachs were hurting.

So, anyway, Jimmy isn't as nice as Dad, but he doesn't tell me off or anything so we are quite lucky. It's great fun stopping at our dad's house though. I get to be a bit more grown up there because he works shifts. This means that I make tea for me and Josh. My speciality is cheese and beans on toast but I'm also pretty good at veggie sausage sandwich. Dad's flat is the downstairs part of an old house. There are three nurses who live upstairs. There's one man and two women. They're very nice. They play music quite loud at night, and sometimes during the day for that matter. It's not a problem though because Josh and I quite like it. It's good when they start talking quite loudly too. You can't quite hear what they are saying but it sounds nice, and when somebody says something funny you can hear them all burst out laughing. It's really good having nurses who live upstairs because they can look after you if you get hurt.

One time, Josh and I were walking home from school. We did something

47

that was really quite naughty. We should not have done it. Snudge had come to meet us from school. She often did that. Josh and I were throwing a ball for her to run and fetch. Well, Josh and I were throwing balls all over the place for her. We were walking down an alleyway that was a bit of a short cut to Dad's flat. I threw a ball and it went over a garden fence. Snudge jumped (or, I suppose you might say half climbed) over the fence and chased after the ball. We heard a splash on the other side of the fence but there was no sign of Snudge re-emerging over the fence. So Josh and I climbed up to look over it, and there was Snudge wringing wet because she had landed in a pond. She stood there shaking herself dry from head to foot. She wagged her tail when she saw us, but she couldn't come away because she hadn't got the ball back. It was balanced in the middle of the pond, resting on a water lily. Poor old Snudge. She had never come back without the ball before and she didn't want to start now. I told Josh to stay where he was and to wait for us. I had decided to help Snudge out and to go and retrieve the ball myself. I was leaning over and trying to drag the ball back with a stick when I heard a sudden thud behind me. It was Josh. He didn't want to be left by himself on the other side of the fence, so he climbed over as well. Snudge was going mad. She was kind of jumping up and down and running around and barking because she was so frustrated at not being able to get to the ball. I told Josh to hold my hand so that I could reach a little further across the water. Snudge kept barking but I told her to be quiet so that the owners of the house didn't come out. Josh was holding onto my hand and I was leaning out. I just managed to knock the ball onto the water but it actually went a little further away instead of falling nearer to us. So I slid my toes a little into the water so that I could reach an extra few centimetres. I told Josh to hold on tight and leant a little further out. But, as you might have guessed, I leant a little too far and my weight made me slip right out of Josh's hand and I fell into the pond. There was a great big splash and I was covered from head to foot in water and I had water lilies and pondweed stuck in my hair and all over my clothes. I spat out a mouthful of pond water and shook myself down just like Snudge did. We heard a man roaring from the house.

He shouted something like, "Who is in my garden? You wait until I get my hands on you!"

I told Snudge to jump back over the fence and she scampered back over

it straight away. I clasped my hands together and gave Josh a leg up and he jumped over to the other side. I started climbing the fence myself and I saw the man come running from the house. He had a bald head and a red face with a big white beard. He was wearing an old vest and some long johns. He had thick grey socks with holes in the toes and he was running towards me. He must have stood on a sharp stone because he let out a huge cry and he started hopping around, holding his foot. I climbed the fence and he grabbed a broom handle and ran towards me. I held onto the top of the fence and dropped down to the other side where Snudge and Josh were waiting for me. I thought that I had made it until I felt a sudden thud come down on my fingers. The old man walloped me across my hand with his broom handle. I had never known pain like it. Me, Josh and Snudge ran off home as fast as we could, but my hand was throbbing like mad. All of my fingers were swelling up and they went a blue and purple colour.

When I got to my dad's flat, he wasn't there. This wasn't unusual because he didn't always finish work at the same time. So I went upstairs to the nurses and I showed them my hand and they made a fuss of me. They put ointment on my hand and made sure

that no fingers were broken. I told them a tall tale about how it happened. I said that I dropped something in an alleyway on the way home and, when I knelt down to try and find it, a teenage boy came along and hit me on the back of my hand with an iron bar. I don't know why I tell tall tales. Sometimes I just do it without thinking and for no good reason at all. Maybe I didn't want to admit that I had gone into a stranger's garden. I don't know, but I know that I told them that tall tale without thinking. They wanted to call the police but I begged them not to. Thankfully they didn't or I would have ended up in a bigger mess trying to explain what happened to the

56

police. When my dad came home, he made a fuss of me as well. He bought us

all chips and Josh kept asking me if I was all right. Snudge kept on trying to lick my face. I think that she felt it was her fault. It wasn't really. It was that stupid old man with the smelly socks. After all, I was only trying to get my ball back. I tried to get a day off school. I told my dad that I couldn't write with a swollen hand, but he said that I would get into too much mischief if I was left alone all day. He was probably right. I mean, look how much trouble I got into just walking home from school by myself.

I was at my dad's flat the day that the biggest thing in my life happened. It was so big that everybody knows about it. The story was in all of the local papers. It was in all of the national papers and it was in the papers in places like America and Australia and Japan. We had television crews camped out all around my dad's flat and we were in every magazine that you could think of.

I had already got a reputation for telling tall tales and, because of that, people naturally thought that I always told tall tales. But I really don't tell tall tales all of the time and what I am about to tell you really did happen.

It all started one evening when Josh and I were at my dad's flat. Dad was in the house watching TV, and Josh and I were trying to mend a puncture in Josh's bicycle tyre. The bike was stood upside down on the path at the back of Dad's flat. We had a bucket of water out and we were sitting on the back step trying to find out where Josh's puncture was.

Snudge was down at the bottom of the garden and we could hear her whimpering. It was as though she was making little crying noises under her breath. We couldn't see her straight away because there's a lawn with a path at the top of the garden and then there is a privet hedge with a gap in it and behind the privet there's a little gazebo where you can sit out on a summer's evening. That evening was quite warm but it was September. It was not quite

summer but it was not quite autumn either.

Snudge came running up the garden to where Josh and I were sitting and we could tell from the way that she was begging with her paws and holding her head that she wanted us to follow her. So we left Josh's puncture and followed Snudge down to the bottom of the garden. What we found there was the most amazing sight that any human being has ever seen.

Dancing in a little circle at the bottom of the garden were six beautiful fairies. Josh and I were open mouthed. We looked at each other and then back at the fairies. They danced and laughed and twinkled in the half light of the late summer evening. They held hands and danced in a circle. They were boy, girl, boy, girl around the circle and they had gold and silver stars sparkling around them. They had dark hair and beautiful dark skin with brilliant white teeth. They wore sparkling silver and gold clothes and they laughed and smiled as they danced. Josh and I were in a trance. We just couldn't believe what we were seeing. Snudge was bursting with excitement. She was half growling and half crying and her tail was wagging backwards and forwards so hard that it made her whole body shake. She was dancing around just as much as the fairies were. Josh and I never said a word. We were so awestruck that we could barely breathe, let alone talk. Then the fairies started fading a little in front of our eyes. We begged them not to go, but they just shrugged their shoulders and carried on dancing. But now, as they danced, they faded a little. We shouted for Dad to come down and see them and, when we started shouting, Snudge started barking and, the more we shouted and screamed for Dad to come out, the more Snudge barked until eventually she was howling like a wolf.

Dad came running out to see what all of the fuss was about and so did

65

the nurses from upstairs. Dad was telling us to calm down. Josh was pulling Dad's arm and dragging him down to where the fairies were. The nurses ran out of the house and joined us. When they got there, the fairies had all faded away. Josh and I were telling them all about the fairies and the way that they were dressed and the way that they danced. Dad told Snudge to stop barking but, no matter how hard she tried, barking and crying noises kept coming out of her mouth and she kept walking around the garden because she was too excited to stand still.

The adults were telling us that we had just imagined it all and, as you might

guess, Dad thought that I was telling a tale, but something happened to make them think again.

The nurses from upstairs had a friend stopping with them and she was a journalist. She told the adults that there might be some truth in the story. Part of her job as a journalist was to read old issues of the newspaper and to write a little article each week about the things that made the news in the years gone by. It turned out that fairies had been seen in this area several times and that the first sighting was over a hundred years ago and, each time, it had been children who had seen the fairies. Each time, the fairies danced and smiled and, each time, they faded away as adults came close. It was amazing. Everything had happened just as it had so many times before. Only this time, it was Josh and I who had witnessed their dance. Oh, and I must remember Snudge as well. She saw them first. If it were not for her, Josh and I may never have got to see them at all.

The next few weeks were like living on a merry-go-round. First of all, we were in the local papers. We had to have our pictures taken, pointing to the place where the fairies had been. Then we were on the radio and we were in the national papers. Then Josh and I went down to

London and we were interviewed on breakfast television. It was the most exciting time of our lives. Dad didn't really mind Josh and me having all of this attention. Mum was against it. She thought it was a tall tale. She said that she expected such things of me, but that it was very naughty to get Josh to tell tall tales as well. I told her over and over again that it was not a tall tale, but she had made her mind up that it was and there was no changing it. Jimmy, Mum's new partner, was dead against us being on TV or on the radio, but Mum said that it was OK.

We even met an old lady who was one hundred and two years old. She had lived in the house where my dad had his flat when she was a little girl. She told us that she had seen the fairies ninety-five years ago when she was a

little girl. She said that she never told anybody about it at first and the fairies came back to see her several times. She said that she had spoken to them and got to know their names. We asked her to tell us their names but she said that she had promised not to tell anybody and she said that she was never going to break that promise as long as she lived. When she did tell her parents about the fairies, her father made her sit in the cupboard under the stairs in the dark. She said that she had been forbidden to ever speak of it again, or else people would come and lock her up in a lunatic asylum. Thank heavens it was different for us.

People did try to make fun of us. It was worse for Josh, really, because the children in my school knew better than to try and pick on me. But whenever anybody started teasing Josh, I soon found out about it and sorted it out. After a while, new reports started appearing in the press and they weren't as nice. Word had got about that I was in the habit of telling tall tales and soon everybody began telling newspaper reporters about some of the tall tales that I had made up. Now I admit that some of them were true, but some people were telling tall tales about me telling tall tales! It was about then that Mum and Jimmy (especially Jimmy, if I'm honest) started getting smug because they said things like "I told you that you shouldn't go talking to the newspapers" or "I said that no good would come of it" or "I knew that this would all end in tears". Anyway, he was wrong there because I wasn't crying and I wasn't sorry either. How could anybody in the world possibly do anything as utterly fantastic as seeing fairies and not tell everyone about it? I know that the old lady didn't tell anybody, but that was because she wasn't allowed to. My heart would dry up and become tired and stop beating if I had to keep a story like that to

74

myself. In a way Jimmy was right, though, because the night that the fairies came to visit us became the most important night of my life. It was the only thing anybody ever wanted to talk to me about. It was the same for Josh and all that anybody really wanted to know was whether it was true or not. But really, that is just what they thought they wanted to know. What they really wanted to know was that it was a tall tale, but they wanted to be the only one who knew that it was a tall tale. They wanted it to be their secret and for everybody else to think that it was true. I've got some advice for you: always try to keep the telling

of tall tales to a minimum. (If you're
anything like me you won't be able to
stop telling them altogether but you can
try doing it as little as possible.) Then
my advice to you would be that you really

76

should believe in fairies. I don't know why they can only be seen by children, but that is just the way it is. I think it is fairly certain to say that if you don't believe in them they won't appear for you. And finally, I think that if you do see them then you should think long and hard about who you tell. The story of how me and Josh and Snudge saw the fairies will be an important part of our lives for as long as we live, but something else happened that was probably even more fantastic than that.

I bet that there will be some people who will read this and think that it's all one big tall tale, but it isn't. This next part of my story is fantastic.

Some time had passed since the incident with the fairies. I had gone into the upper juniors and Josh had started in year three. I told my teacher that I had a wonderful tale to tell in Show-and-Tell. She asked me if it was a true story or if it was a tall tale. Honestly! The cheek of it! She doesn't ask anybody else if their stories are true. I told her that it was most definitely true. I don't know why I said that because it was not true at all. So this meant that I had already told one tall tale and I was about to tell another. In our class, we all sit round the teacher's chair on a carpet when it's time for Show-and-Tell. It's a bit like the start of a literacy lesson. I knew that mine was going to be the best tell.

There was another boy who was showing a tarantula spider skin. Honestly, he just stood there with it in a box. I mean: what kind of a Show-and-Tell is that? If I had a tarantula skin, my tell would have been brilliant. I would have told them how my whole family spent four hours looking for a tarantula that had escaped from our next-door neighbour's spider collection. Then I would have said that we all had to sleep in the same bed because we were so afraid of it. I would have told how the spider was bird-eating and poisonous. Then I would have told them that we woke up in the morning and the only evidence that we found about the spider was that it shed its skin on our pillow. Then I'd tell them that there could be spider eggs all over the place and that they were only tiny so I could have carried them into school without even knowing. Now that's a Show-and-Tell. Honestly, how boring can somebody get to just stand there and show a spider skin with no story! I couldn't live like that. Stories are the best things in the world.

I'm afraid that my story was a bit on the tall side. I reminded everybody about Betty, the old lady who used to live in the house where my dad lives now.

I told them that I had visited her over the weekend and that I had talked to her about the fairies that we had both seen. I could see that the teacher wasn't very pleased with me talking about the fairies. She didn't stop me, though.

Betty said that she wanted to share her experience with me. I told them all about the old folks' home where she lived and how Betty seemed to be very eager to let everybody know the things that she wasn't allowed to talk about when she was a child. This might seem strange to you, but I got a feeling that the fairies that she was talking about were exactly the same ones that Josh and I had seen. I don't mean

similar ones, but actually the same ones.

She saw them more often than us. To

begin with they just danced and laughed

without talking but after a while they jumped up on the garden furniture and they flew around in circles and then they landed on her shoulder and then they sprinkled fairy dust in the air and disappeared. She always knew when the fairies were going to call, because the cat made strange noises and her hair used to stand up on her back. Nobody else knew what this meant except for Betty, so she used to wait until nobody was looking at her and then she would sneak down to the bottom of the garden and visit them. I know just how she must have felt. The only person in the whole world that the fairies were visiting was her. She told me that they never had proper conversations with her, but they used to say some things like: "Always remember to smile. When you smile you make your star shine brighter". They told her that every boy and girl has a star and it grows as they grow. The more you smile the brighter your star shines. Then when you die, God puts you inside the star and you shine forever in the sky.

To be honest, I thought about this tall tale a bit too much. I had spoken to the old lady about the fairies shortly after Josh and I had seen them. Then, lately, I had thought about this tall tale, and then the truth and the tall tale had kind of merged and so I couldn't really remember what was the truth and what was a tall tale. Anyway, I told the whole class about the visit, but our teacher questioned me about it. It was obvious that she thought that the whole visit was a tall tale. Of course, I didn't like that very much, so I told her that it was true and that I could prove it was true because the old lady had told me that she wanted to come and visit our class. I was usually very good when it came to telling tall tales, but, to be honest, that was one of the most stupid things that I had ever said. The teacher thought that it would be a great idea for the old lady to come and talk to the children. This was awful. I had gone too far. Now I had to find a way of explaining why the old lady couldn't come into school. I told the teacher that I would go back to the old lady and arrange for her to come into school. I didn't know what I was going to do. I wracked my brains for days trying to think of a really good tall tale to get me out of the awful mess that I had got myself into.

Then a brilliant idea came to me and I knew that I would be able to come out of this smelling of roses. That is, if I could pull off this most wonderful of plans. My idea was this: I decided to go to the old people's home and talk to Betty and put the idea into her mind that she might like to come and visit my school.

When I arrived at the home, the old lady was just finishing her tea so I sat aside and waited for a while. Everybody was very kind. As they walked past, nearly everybody stopped to chat to me. They all asked who I was visiting and, one by one, they all warned me not to take too much notice of the stories she was likely to tell me. Do you know, I think that they suspected her of telling tall tales? I went into her room and sat down on the stool beside her comfy chair. She was really pleased to see me. She told me that it was a good job that I didn't come a week earlier because she had been on her holidays. I was really pleased about this because I was a little bit worried that she might

be too old to visit places. As she began to tell me about her holiday, I soon realised that she loved to travel. Her holiday had been to Scotland. She loved to travel by train and she told me all about her love of the Scottish Highlands. I could see that talking about Scotland was making her very happy. She talked about walking in the hills and camping out in the way that she had done since she was a child. She told me that she always went back to a place called Loch Ness. Her eyes became watery as she mentioned her favourite holiday destination. My ears pricked up, because I knew Loch Ness. Then I sort of froze a bit inside, because I could guess what was coming next. I bet you have guessed too, haven't you? Well, I'm sure that you have guessed right, because she told me that she kept going back year after year because she wanted more than anything to see the Loch Ness Monster one more time before she died. Now I know that I am the last person to say this, but I was afraid that she was about to tell me one of the tallest tales in history. She told me that she was on holiday in Loch Ness when she was a teenage girl. She went for a long late night stroll on the banks of the Loch. She was all by herself and a bright full moon lit up the water. She heard a rumbling sound coming

from deep below the Loch and waves of water began to ride up like a huge sea-side wave. Then she saw the second most amazing sight of her life. Nessy, the Loch Ness Monster, rose up out of the water. She was a huge green monster that looked a bit like a massive sea dinosaur. Betty said that Nessy looked straight at her and then she let out an enormous squealing kind of a roar. Steam came out of her ears and she winked an eye straight at Betty. Then she turned round and swam back down into the deep. Just before she went below the water, she waved her gigantic tail in the air and then she disappeared and was gone. Betty hoped that she had

not submerged forever and so she returned there each year in the hope that she might see her again.

I decided not to ask her to come and talk to our class. They might think that Nessy was just a tall tale. I made my mind up to tell my teacher that Betty was unable to make any travel arrangements for a while. I said goodbye to Betty and left. The matron reminded me not to take too much notice of the stories that Betty told. I told her that I was just pleased that I didn't visit her the week before when she was on her holiday. The matron just smiled and shook her head. She said that was a silly thing to say because Betty had not had a holiday for fifteen years. I felt great. I wondered if I would still be telling tall tales when I was over a hundred years old.

The teacher soon forgot about Betty coming to visit anyway. This was good because it meant I never had to dream up another tall tale. Mostly, I tried to avoid telling tall tales for the rest of the school year. Sometimes I was more successful than others.

One day, I never had to ask the teacher if I could do a Show-and-Tell. She asked me! To be honest, everybody who saw me asked me what had happened to me. I had a really bad black eye and all of my cheek was bruised and battered. I told the teacher what had happened and she asked me to stand in front of the whole class and tell them the story. Well, obviously I didn't need to be asked twice because you know how much I love telling stories. Everybody knew that this really did happen to me during the night before because I left school on the previous day without a mark on me. I told them all about my very eventful trip to the swimming pool the night before. I am really good at swimming and I had a contest with my dad to see who could swim the furthest. I'm a really good swimmer and I won. You never know with my dad if he's letting you win or not, but I am a really good swimmer, honestly, so it could be true that I really can swim further than him. When we were walking home, I lagged behind Dad and Josh. I was a bit tired because I had worn myself out by swimming so much. We were walking along some wasteland to take a short cut home. Josh and Dad decided that they would play a trick on me by hiding behind some garages. I was doing absolutely nothing, I swear! I was just walking along, minding my own business, when a teenage boy who was walking past picked up an iron bar and hit me around the face. I swear I didn't do anything to make him do it. It all

happened really quickly, but he ran off
and I screamed out. Dad and Josh came

running back to me. Josh was crying more than I was. There's a chip shop by the wasteland near to my dad's flat. Two policemen were just going to get some chips and they saw what happened. One came over to see if I was all right and the other chased after the boy. I was able to point to where he went.

The wasteland that we walk across to get home was used by a lot of teenagers, especially boys, because they have made their own scrambling course and they ride their motor bikes all around it. The wasteland is by a wood called the Enchanted Wood. The boy ran off as far as I could see and I think he was heading round the other side of the wood.

I was OK. I was able to walk so they didn't need to call an ambulance. The police took me to the hospital in their police car. I had to wait around for ages. They would not let me go home because they said that they needed to make sure that I didn't go dizzy and start feeling sick. I had to make a statement to the police because they caught the boy who did it. It's a shame that the attack had hurt me so much because it was a brilliant night. The nurses who live upstairs from my dad let me sit in the nurses' private lounge where normal members of the public are not allowed. The police were really cool as well because they let me start the siren off on their car. It was a really amazing night but because of the swimming and everything I was really tired.

Dad said that I could stay off school but I didn't want to. Anyway, it was really good being in school because everybody made a fuss of me because my face was all black and blue. My teacher even gave me a special award in the "Praise Assembly" for being so brave and coming into school. My bruises soon cleared up. I heal really quickly, I always have. Everything was fine until parents' day when the teacher told Mum and Dad how brave I had been. My parents couldn't understand it because my version of what happened was not entirely true. In fact, it was a teensy bit of a tall tale. The part about us going swimming was true except we never actually got as far as the pool. My dad was hitching his bag up onto his shoulder and I was standing behind him. The corner of his bag had a metal bit on it and that caught me under the eye. It didn't really hurt that much, but it did cause me to have a big black eye and I had all of that purple and red bruising all around my cheek.

I said "sorry" to everyone. But, honestly, some people really make a fuss

103

about things. I don't really understand why people (especially adults) get so cross. I mean, at the end of the day, it was only a tall tale. I mean, it's not really the end of the world, is it? It's not as though I've hurt anyone or stolen anything. A tall tale is just a tall tale! Normally, the only person who gets hurt is me and that's only because nobody believes me even when I'm telling the truth. That happens to me a lot and it's really annoying!

I often go and sit down at the bottom of the garden to see if the fairies might come back. I'm so glad that Josh was with me. There's a part of me that wishes that somebody else could be with me when they visit again, but, for the most part, I don't care what other people think. I'm glad that they only came for me and Josh. Well, actually, they didn't only come to see me and Josh, they came to Snudge as well. So really, I owe the most important moment of my life to her. If she hadn't seen them in the first place, and fetched me and Josh, the fairies could have come to the bottom of our garden and we would never have seen them.

I'll tell you something else that's true about Snudge. She nearly died once in the winter. I'll tell you this true tale about Snudge and it might save your life. We went tobogganing one day.

There were four of us. There was me and Josh and Dad and Snudge. We had a really good time. It was just before Christmas and there was about a metre of snow everywhere. It was set to be the first white Christmas in years. When we woke up, we couldn't believe our eyes. It was like a Christmas card. There was just one complete layer of snow everywhere you looked. An announcement came on the radio to say all the schools in the city were closed for the day because of the snow. It was a Thursday, so we were at our dad's house. It was Dad who came up with the idea of tobogganing. He wasn't going to work until late in the afternoon. Dad phoned up Mum and said he would take us up to the hills and then he would go off to work and I would take Josh and Snudge down to Mum's house later.

We had a brilliant time. Snudge was not big enough to walk around in the snow without getting virtually buried in it. So she stayed up on a lookout wall and just watched us. We messed around on the toboggan, having fun. It was mostly falling off, to be honest. We had loads of fun and we made a huge giant snowman. When it was time for us to go, we walked down the hill together and then me, Josh and Snudge had to go one way and Dad went the other.

Now this is the part of the story
that could save your life. There's a

duck pond that we pass on the way home and it was completely frozen over. (There were no ducks there. I wonder where they go when it freezes?) Some children had made a slide on it and they were sliding on it for ages. It was the best slide that Josh and I had ever seen in our lives and so we decided to join them. We called Snudge to come and join in but she wouldn't come. She stood on the side and sort of did a dance and growled and barked. I went over and picked her up and carried her onto the ice. She sort of whimpered a little bit and cried but when I put her down she stopped. She didn't exactly start running around but she did walk slowly around and she kept looking around her as though she had suddenly found herself standing in mid air. She was looking to see where the floor had gone. We ran around and slid all over the place. It was brilliant. We had lots of fun and there were about ten other kids playing on the ice at the same time. Snudge wasn't happy, though. She kept walking closer to the edge of the pond and she was sort of barking a little bark to try and get us to go on the land. It was similar to the way she got us to go to the fairies. Well, it was obvious that she never wanted to stay on the ice. To be honest, she never wanted to go on the ice in the first place.

We decided to go home because Snudge was so upset. The ice by the edge of the pond had thawed a bit and so Josh and I jumped over it and called Snudge to follow us. She couldn't do it though. She just pawed the ice a bit and whimpered. I couldn't understand why she was so frightened. I had seen her jump over garden fences in the past, so I knew that she could have easily jumped over the little bit of thawing ice by the side of the pond. Josh and I called her again and you could see that she was making her mind up to try and jump it. She walked back a few paces and tried to run but she couldn't get any grip with her paws so she was unable to make a proper lift off and she slipped off the end of the ice and into the freezing water. Josh screamed and I fell to the ground and reached out my arms. I just managed to grab hold of Snudge's collar as she was going under the water for the second time and I dragged her to the side. Snudge was absolutely freezing and if she had stayed under the water for another few seconds then she might have died. Actually, she would have almost certainly died. We shouted to the other children who were still on the ice and told them to get off, but, do you know, they still carried on playing on the ice even though I told them that our dog had nearly died and that their lives were in danger.

We were able to get Snudge dry and she was back to her normal self before too long. So that was a true tale with a happy ending but, whenever I think about how close Snudge came to dying, it sends a shiver all the way through me. I also realise that I could have died myself or even Josh could have died and I am supposed to look after Josh. I know this now: playing on frozen ice can kill you. That's why I told you that this story could save your life. I hope that you will learn from my mistake and never go near frozen ponds. I never volunteered to tell this story in Show-

and-Tell. I was worried my mum and dad would find out that I hadn't gone straight home.

But I never learnt how to suddenly become the kind of kid who does everything that she should do. Well, I've never claimed to be a little angel, have I? For some reason, I have to do things that look as though they might be a bit of an adventure. It's being like this that brought about the most amazing tale of my life. It started out in a really ordinary way, the way that most great stories do. It was about six months after the stupid day I took Josh and Snudge onto the frozen pond. The weather couldn't have been more different. It had been a blazing hot summer's day and we were at our dad's flat. We had come home from school in the normal way but Dad wasn't there. He had left us a note, which told us to go upstairs and see the nurses. So we went upstairs to see them and they told us that Dad had been called into work. They do that sometimes. He works different shifts. Sometimes he starts work at six o'clock in the morning and sometimes he starts work at two in the afternoon. When he is working a late shift, he starts work at ten o'clock at night. Normally when we are with him, he is there all of the time, so this was unusual. The nurses said that we could stay with them or we could stay in Dad's flat and just call up to them if we needed anything. We decided that we would stay downstairs.

Josh watched telly for a bit and I did my homework. To be honest, I'm pretty good at school and I like doing homework. My homework that night was to write a story. Well, I think stories are the best thing in the world, and I write stories just for fun, so I couldn't be happier when we get one to do for homework. We got a phone call from Dad, who told us that he was having a break from work. He told us to meet him at the Enchanted chip shop for tea. The Enchanted is the best chip shop in the world. We are not allowed to go every week but we would if we could. To be honest, Josh and I would be happy to eat at the Enchanted every night if we were allowed to. I always have chips and mushy peas.

Me and Josh and Snudge set off for the chip shop. It was a beautiful evening. I love summer's evenings. I always throw a ball for Snudge as we walk down the road. We could hear the local church bellringers practise as we passed by a man who was cutting his lawn. Summer sounds are the best sounds in the world. And the smell of freshly mown grass is the best smell in the world. I was throwing the ball for Snudge and she was jumping around at her very best. She was doing somersaults in the air and jumping over garden walls. We couldn't play around too much though because we only had about ten minutes to get to the chip shop. Dad had phoned the nurses and told them that we were allowed to go. When we got to the chip shop, Dad was waiting for us. He said sorry to us over and over again but there was no need to, really. Josh and I were perfectly happy being by ourselves and we felt safe because we knew that the nurses were upstairs if we needed them.

The chip shop is opposite some wasteland that backs onto the

Enchanted Wood. That's where the chip shop gets its name from. The Enchanted Wood is out of bounds. We are not allowed in it. The wood is closed to the public. The story that everybody tells about the wood is that, if anybody is in there when the clock turns twelve o'clock midnight, then they will be turned into a statue of gold. Nobody really knows if it's true but everyone tells the same story. There is even a sign outside the wood warning the public not to go in. People do use the wasteland, though. There are some little hills with benches on and people sit there to eat their chips. That's where we ate ours. There were quite a few teenagers there as well. They use the wasteland to play with their scramblers. They have races over a course that they've made and some of them race mountain bikes too and they try to do wheelies. I love summer evenings when there are people out doing things and enjoying themselves.

Dad was in a really good mood considering he had to do extra work on a beautiful summer's night. When we finished our chips, he gave Josh a piggy back over to the bin. There were two bins, one on either side of the chip shop, and Dad ran from one to the other and back and Josh threw the papers in the bin. Summer evenings are great. I know that there are some really nice things about the winter. It's great to make snowmen and throw snowballs and stuff but when you get a beautiful warm summer's evening, I think that it's the best time in the whole world. Dad set off back to work and told us to go straight home.

I think you know me well enough now to know that I don't always do what I should do. I don't plan to do things that I shouldn't do, but sometimes I just drift into doing them.

After Dad left, and Josh and I were walking along the side of the wasteland, we saw some older kids that we knew. They shouted over to say hello

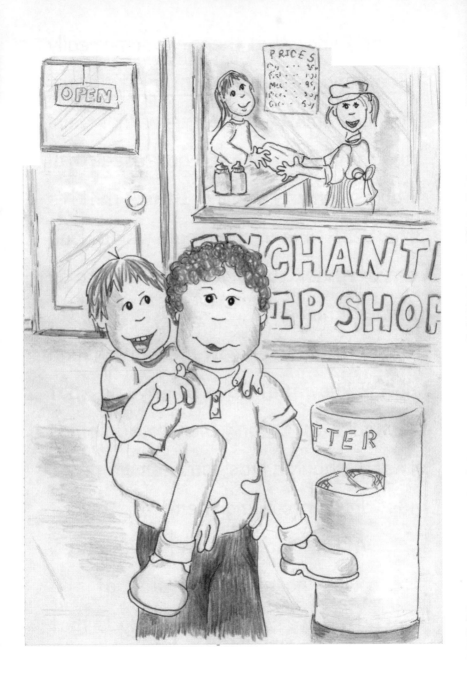

and I got Josh to stop and look at them on their bikes. Josh wanted to go home. He's a good kid. I'm going to make an effort to be more like him in the future. I told him that we should stay for a while and watch the teenagers doing their tricks. I promised him that we wouldn't stay for long and, when we did go home, we would go straight home. He didn't mind much. He doesn't complain. Some little brothers are always crying or they are having tantrums or saying that there is something wrong with this or with that. Josh isn't like that, I promise. He's just a really good kid. We sat and watched our friends for a while. We were cheering them on and Josh jumped up and down every time one of them did something good. It was one of those summer nights where the sky goes a beautiful colour of red and orange and we could hear the church bellringers practising their tunes. It was a great night. Everybody was laughing and having fun. Snudge was running up and down the side of the track. She dodged from side to side and chased her tail around from time to time. I've never seen her so happy.

Then one of the girls offered me her bike to have a go. It was brilliant. I didn't need to be asked twice. The course was a bit tricky. There were some sharp turns and a couple of quite high jumps. I wasn't scared, though. I knew that I could do at least as well as the other kids. I jumped onto the bike and did a little bit of a practice run up and down. It felt great. When you slammed the brakes on and did a sharp turn all the dust from the dry ground flew up into the air and it looked like something from a film. It was brilliant. I flew around the course like my life depended upon it and I went straight into second place. It was just the best feeling. Everybody was cheering for me. Once I got my breath back and rested for a while, we decided to have a race between me and the boy who was in the lead. Josh had forgotten all about us being out late without permission. I don't think I have ever seen him so happy. He sat on the hill by the side of the track and shouted me on. Snudge sat on his lap with her head on his knees. She didn't stay there for long though. She was more excited than me and Josh. She was jumping up and down as if the ground was too hot for her to stand on. Her tongue was hanging out of her mouth the way that dogs' tongues do when they are running around too much on hot days. I love it when dogs are happy and they wag their tail so much that they catch sight of it out of the corner of their eyes and then they start chasing it. I wasn't fast enough to beat the best bike rider but

I had a great time trying. It was getting late and everybody started drifting off. Josh was getting tired and so I told him that we would go home too. I put my arm around him. He is the cutest little brother in the world and he gets even cuter when he's tired.

We did a lot of smiling that night. Our stars must have been getting brighter all the time. You could see a few stars in the darkening sky. I asked Josh if ours were out tonight, and he said they should be because they were the brightest stars in the sky. I hugged him tighter still. I love him when he says nice things like that. Snudge started jumping up at my pocket. She wanted me to get the ball and throw it for her. I wanted to throw it for her, but I could see that Josh was really tired and besides it had got dark very quickly. We were supposed to have been home ages ago. Josh could see that I wanted to throw it for her so he told me that I could do it. I threw it as far as I could and Snudge went flying after it. I was amazed that she had any energy left after all of the running and jumping around that she had been doing. Josh ran off and I threw the ball to him and Snudge raced after it and got to it before it reached him. Then she ran over to him and dropped it for Josh to throw. Josh wound his arm up like a baseball player and then swung himself around and around before he let go of the ball. Josh can really throw a ball a long way and it went into the Enchanted Wood. Snudge raced off and jumped over the little fence by the outside trees. In the briefest of seconds, she was completely out of sight. Josh and I raced to the edge of the wood and peered in amongst the trees to try and see her. Normally Snudge would never go near the Enchanted Wood, but she's mad about getting a ball when you've thrown it for her.

Josh and I walked up and down to see if we could see her, but the trees were too thick. All of the trees had grown so close together, all you could see was darkness. We called her to come back, but she didn't come. We couldn't even hear her moving about, so we began to get quite worried. I told Josh that I was going in to look for her. There was a look of terror in his eyes. Nobody ever went into the Enchanted Wood and, if you were even going to think about it, you certainly would not dream of going in at night time. Josh pulled my arm back and reminded me about the legend. Like I needed to be reminded! I couldn't leave Snudge in there alone though. I told Josh to stay exactly where he was and not to go anywhere. To be honest, he looked too frightened to move very far.

I climbed over the fence and started making my way through the trees. I kept calling Snudge as I went, but I couldn't hear her. As I got further and further into the forest, the whole place got darker. I kept calling out to Josh as well to make sure that he was all right. He kept calling back to let me know he was OK. I felt really sorry for him, having to wait all by himself. I called out to Snudge again and then I heard her whimpering. Tears came to my eyes because she sounded as though she was in pain. I imagined her being caught in a trap or having a broken leg or something. I started to fight my way towards her. The trees had huge great roots that had grown up above the ground and were strangling each other. The low branches were thick and heavy and were so overgrown that they could not be separated from the roots. Some trees had fallen over and were living on their sides. I went around trees whenever I could and wrestled through them where I could see the smallest of gaps that I might be able to get through. My t-shirt was all scratched and I had little scratch marks on my arms and legs. I crawled under one branch that was very low and near to the ground but the tree was too large for me to get my legs through and I got myself stuck. I was facing the ground and, even when I forced my eyes upwards, I couldn't see any sky at all. It had gone really dark and the wood was overgrown with trees. No matter how hard I tried, I couldn't move forwards or backwards. I was well and truly stuck. I called out to Josh to make sure he was all right, but he had moved. His voice was much further away. He was far away to my right even though he had been level with me when I started out. I told him off for moving, but he told me that he had stayed still and that it was me who had moved. I didn't know what to do. I couldn't tell him that I was stuck because he would only get frightened, and, anyway, there was nothing he could do.

I could hear Snudge moving around. She wasn't hurt. She must have been stuck and couldn't get back to me. That must have been what was making her whimper. I just stayed where I was, thinking, because I couldn't do anything else. I don't know how long I was there for but it seemed like a long time.

Josh came looking for me. I sent him back. I told him to wait outside for me, but he knew something was wrong. I could hear him getting closer to me, so I kept calling out to him, so that he would know which direction to go in. He's got a lot of guts for a little kid. I heard Snudge barking. She was getting closer to me as well. Josh reached me first and he started pulling branches away that were trapping me in. Once he moved them just a few centimetres, I was able to force my legs free. Then Snudge arrived. We were all together at last, and Josh and I sat on the ground to rest for a minute and Snudge went between us licking our faces. It was very late now. Even when we could see the sky all we could see was darkness and stars. Josh asked me if we would all be turned to statues of gold if we were still in the wood after it turned midnight. I gave him a hug and told him not to worry. I told him that it was probably a tall tale. We didn't know what time it was, but it was very late indeed.

I will be honest and admit that I was a bit worried about being turned to gold. You would really have to live near the Enchanted Wood to know what it's like. Everybody, and I mean absolutely everybody, tells the story and you hear it so often that you can end up believing it a little bit. But right now I was much more worried about being out on our own so late. I kept on thinking what Dad would say if he were to find out that we hadn't gone home straight away but had stayed out

playing. That would make him mad enough, but if he were to find out we had gone into the Enchanted Wood as well, then he would probably have a fit.

We got up to leave and I went first. I kept a hold of Josh's hand and Snudge followed close behind. If I had to climb over thick branches I made sure that I got Josh over too. He was really tired by now and he was finding it harder to get out than he did to get in. I made sure that I kept an eye on Snudge as well. When she needed a bit of help, I picked her up and made it as easy as I could for her. It was a lot harder to get out, though, because it had got so dark we could see virtually nothing at all. I got really annoyed because I saw a dead tree on its side that we had passed some time earlier, so I knew that we had been going around in circles for a while.

It occurred to me that Dad never said what time he was working until. I had a dreadful thought that he might be at home waiting for us and worrying about us. I made myself a promise that I would never do anything like this again. If I were ever told to go anywhere straight away, I would go there straight away. I thought about how sad Dad would be if he was at home waiting for us and not knowing where we were. I made a really serious promise to myself that I would try my very hardest never to do something that might make him sad again.

We carried on trying to get to the outside of the wood for a while and then something really good happened. I heard a car in the distance, so I knew that we were heading in the right direction and that we would soon be free. We started trying harder than ever. We climbed over branches, stepped our way over the huge enlarged roots and dragged ourselves up steep banks. Then we looked through a gap in the trees and saw a light in the distance. This was fantastic! We only had about fifty metres to go and then we would be free. Just then the church bells rang.

The midnight bells. We had to get out of there before the bell chimed for the twelfth time because if we were still inside we would be turned into statues of gold. I made my way as fast as I could to the little outside fence that went all around the edge of the wood. I was dragging poor Josh behind me as though he were a rag doll. The bells chimed on seven, eight, nine.

The fence was just metres away. I brushed myself past the final tree just as the bells chimed for the eleventh time and I pulled Josh over with me. We were free at last and we hadn't been turned into gold! A second or two later Snudge came tumbling out as well. We were all free! It was brilliant! But we were still in a lot of trouble. It was midnight. It was pitch black. We could barely see our hands in front of our faces and we still had to get ourselves home. We were all very tired, but we made our way home as quickly as we could. When we got there, we were in luck. Dad was still at work. We decided to go straight to bed. We were exhausted and, to be honest, we had lived through enough excitement not only for one night but for a whole lifetime.

I was woken up in the morning by Dad shouting up the stairs.

"Tanya," he said, "Can you come down here at once, please? There's

some explaining I would like you to do."

My heart sank. I knew that it was too much to hope for that we could have been so naughty and still be able to avoid getting caught. I decided to confess everything and tell the whole truth from beginning to end. I wasn't going to let Josh take the blame for anything because he couldn't have gone home by himself so none of it was his fault. I went downstairs and Dad was standing there waiting for me.

He said, "Can you explain this?"

Then he opened up the kitchen door and there was Snudge. Her tail had turned gold! She looked up at me and wagged her new tail and I looked at

Dad and shrugged my shoulders. Then Josh came down and pulled his way between our legs.

When he saw Snudge's tail he said, "Wow!"

I told Josh that it was probably the strangest tail in the whole world. Then I squeezed his hand.

Josh said, "Yes, I think it probably is."

Also by the same author...

Harriet the Horrible

E.R.Reilly

Harriet is a lovely little girl- that is until she
gets upset. Then she dreams up wonderfully
wicked plans to get her own back...Watch out!
That's when nice little Harriet becomes
... Harriet the Horrible!

Harriet the Horrible

in

Best Friends

E.R.Reilly

Harriet and Salty have always got up to lots of mischief but now they are joined by a new girl in school.
Colleen is Harriet's new best friend and toether they have a very special mission in life...

One boy,
One dream,
One club...

Man U? Villa? Everton? Liverpool? Leeds? Arsenal? Chelsea?

E.R.Reilly

This is the story of one boy's dream to be a professional footballer. It is a roller-coaster ride of a book that reaches out to everybody who has ever had a dream.

RASHNU

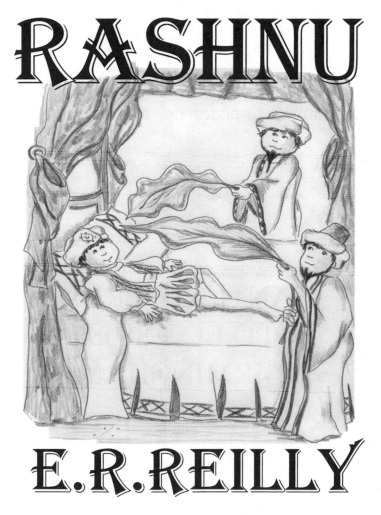

E.R.REILLY

Rashnu is the richest young prince in the whole wide world. He has everything any child could wish for... except friends to play with.

This is the story of how Rashnu searches for friendship.

Contact us to order any of these titles.

SANTIAGO PRESS
PO BOX 8808
BIRMINGHAM
B30 2LR

santiago@reilly19.freeserve.co.uk